Produced by Kroha Associates, Inc.
Middletown, Connecticut.

Printed in the United States of America.

ISBN 1-56326-102-2

Minnie's New Bike

By Ruth Lerner Perle

One day, as Minnie was about to go to the park, a big red delivery truck stopped in front of her house.

Minnie watched the driver as he took a large cardboard box out of the truck.

"I wonder what's in that package," Minnie said to herself.

The driver carried the box to Minnie's door.

"Package for Minnie Mouse," he said with a smile. "Looks like someone is getting a very special surprise."

Minnie looked at the tag on the box. "It's from my favorite aunt," she said. "She always sends me the best presents."

The driver helped Minnie unpack the box. Inside it was the most beautiful bike Minnie had ever seen. It was bright pink with a violet seat, and it had colorful streamers dangling from the handlebars. The handlebars also had a basket and a shiny bell attached to them.

"Well, you sure are a lucky girl," the driver said. "I know a lot of kids who would love to have a bike like this. I hope you enjoy it!"

After the driver left, Minnie examined every part of her wonderful new bicycle.

"This is absolutely the best bike I have ever seen," Minnie said to herself. "Nobody I know has a bike like this! Just wait until I show it to Daisy and Penny!"

Minnie jumped on her bike and started pedaling toward the park. Whee! She pedaled faster and faster, ringing the bell and waving whenever she saw someone she knew.

When Minnie got to the park, Penny and Daisy came running up to her.

"Wow! Where did you get that super bike?" Penny shouted.

"Is it yours?" Daisy wanted to know.

"Yes," Minnie said. "My aunt sent it to me. It's mine, all mine!"

"Can we take turns riding it?" Daisy asked.

"Well, er...uh...I don't know!" Minnie stammered. "The bike is all new and shiny. I'm afraid it might get dirty or else the paint might get scratched. Besides, I haven't really had a chance to ride it much myself."

"Please let us ride it!" Penny cried. "We'll be very careful."
"We'll just go a little way up the path and then come right back!"
Daisy said.

"Maybe I'll let you ride my bike some other time," Minnie said. She got back on her bike and pedaled away.

Daisy and Penny watched Minnie ride away.

"It's not very nice of Minnie not to let us have a turn!" Penny said. "It's not like her to be so selfish."

"She can keep her silly old bike!" Daisy said.

Minnie rode all around the park, but something was wrong.
She still liked her bike, but riding it wasn't so much fun anymore.
She kept thinking of Penny and Daisy.

When Minnie came back around the path, she saw Penny and Daisy sitting under a tree together. They were laughing and talking to each other.

It's no fun being by myself, Minnie thought to herself.

She rode around behind the tree and called, "Hey, you two! What's up?"

Daisy and Penny turned around. "Oh, Minnie! We're so glad you came back," they cried. "We were hoping we could try your bike."

Penny jumped up and said, "Will you let me ride your new bike now? I promise to be very, very careful with it."

Minnie got off the bike. "Well, okay, Penny," she said, "but you'd better be careful."

Penny jumped on the bike and rode up and down the path. When she came back she shouted, "This bike is great! You're so lucky to have it, Minnie."

It's hard to share my brand-new bike, but it was harder to miss out on fun with my friends.

Daisy took her turn next. She rode up the path, but before she knew it, she was headed for a great big mud puddle.

Splash! Minnie's bike was covered with mud.

"Oh, no!" Daisy cried. "Look what I did!"

Minnie came running over. She looked at her muddy bike and her heart sank.

"I'm so sorry, Minnie," Daisy said. "It was an accident. I'll wash your bike for you so it will look new and shiny again."

"I know you must be very angry," Penny said.

"Well, I am a little upset," Minnie admitted.

Then she saw how unhappy Daisy looked and said, "Cheer up, everybody! The bike is a little muddy, but we can still ride it! Who wants to go first?"

Penny and Daisy clapped their hands.

"Thank you, Minnie," Daisy said. "The bike is wonderful! But most wonderful of all is having a friend like you. I found that out today."

Minnie smiled at her friends and said, "I found out something today, too. When you share what you have with friends, it's not half the fun — it's twice the fun!"